P9-DEC-831

In a high-rise building
deep in the heart of a big city
live two private eyes:
Bunny Brown and Jack Jones.
Bunny is the brains,
Jack is the snoop,
and together they
crack cases wide open . . .

This is the story of
Case Number 004:
THE CASE OF
THE TROUBLESOME TURTLE.

story by
Cynthia Rylant

pictures by
G. Brian Karas

To Samantha Wills
—C.R.

To the Chancellor Livingston School
—G.B.K.

Acrylic, gouache, and pencil were used for the full-color art.
The text type is Times.

HarperCollins®, ☕®, Harper Trophy®, and I Can Read Book®
are trademarks of HarperCollins Publishers Inc.

The High-Rise Private Eyes: The Case of the Troublesome Turtle
Text copyright © 2001 by Cynthia Rylant
Illustrations copyright © 2001 by G. Brian Karas
Manufactured in China.
For information address HarperCollins Children's Books, a division of
HarperCollins Publishers, 10 East 53rd Street, New York, NY 10022.
All rights reserved.
www.harperchildrens.com

Library of Congress Cataloging-in-Publication Data
Rylant, Cynthia.
The high-rise private eyes : the case of the troublesome turtle /
by Cynthia Rylant; illustrated by G. Brian Karas.
      p.   cm.
"I Can Read Books."
Summary: Bunny and Jack, animal detectives, investigate the
disappearance of the balloons from the neighborhood toy store.
ISBN 0-688-16312-2 (trade) — ISBN 0-688-16311-4 (lib. bdg.) —
ISBN 0-06-001323-0 (pbk.)
[1. Animals—Fiction. 2. Balloons—Fiction. 3. Football—Fiction.
4. Mystery and detective stories.]
I. Karas, G. Brian, ill. II. Title.
PZ7.R982 Hq 2001   [E]—dc21   00-044271

First Harper Trophy Edition, 2002
Originally published by Greenwillow Books, an imprint of
HarperCollins *Publishers*, in 2001.
11 12 13 SCP 10 9 8
❖

Contents

Chapter 1
Painting

Bunny enjoyed painting on Sundays.

"Why don't you paint me?"

asked Jack.

"Because you won't sit still,"

said Bunny.

"Yes, I will," said Jack.

"No, you won't," said Bunny.

"Will," said Jack.

"Won't," said Bunny.

"Let's just *try*," said Jack.

"I'll be as still as that apple."

"Oh, all right," said Bunny.

"Just sit on that chair there.

And don't move."

"Goody," said Jack.

8

He sat on the chair.

Bunny began to paint.

"Uh-oh," said Jack.

"What?" asked Bunny.

"My nose itches," said Jack.

"Don't scratch," said Bunny.

"Okay," said Jack.

He didn't scratch.

But he turned all red from wanting to.

Bunny kept painting.

"Uh-oh," said Jack again.

"What?" asked Bunny.

"Now my chin itches," said Jack.

"Don't scratch," said Bunny.

"Okay," said Jack.

10

He didn't scratch.

But his eyes bugged out

from wanting to.

Bunny kept painting.

"Uh-oh," said Jack a third time.

"What now?" asked Bunny.

"Now my toe itches," said Jack.

"Don't scratch," said Bunny.

"Okay," said Jack.

He didn't scratch.

But his fur stood on end

from wanting to.

Finally Bunny was finished.

"Okay, all done," she said.

"Thank goodness," said Jack,

scratching like crazy.

"I was about to scream."

"Silly," said Bunny.

"Can I see?" asked Jack.

"Sure," said Bunny.

Jack looked at the painting.

"AAAAGGGGHHHHH!" Jack screamed.

"Goodness," said Bunny.

"Do I really look like that?"
asked Jack.

"Only if you need to scratch,"
said Bunny.

"I never knew
how important scratching is,"
said Jack.

"I'm going to scratch more often."

"Okay," said Bunny.

"Five times a day," said Jack.

"Fine," said Bunny.

"Now I know why you

like to paint apples," said Jack.

"Why?" asked Bunny.

"Because they don't itch," said Jack.

"Bingo," said Bunny.

"I will never ask you

to paint me again," said Jack.

"Okay," said Bunny.

"But could you scratch my back?"
asked Jack.

"Right here, where I can't reach?"

"Oh, for goodness' sake," said Bunny.

Chapter 2
The Case

Bunny and Jack were just about
to go out to lunch when someone
knocked on Bunny's door.
It was Mr. Paris, who owned
the toy store across the street.
"Hello, Mr. Paris!" said Bunny.

"Hello, Bunny. Hello, Jack,"
said Mr. Paris. "I think I need
a private eye. Somebody keeps
taking my balloons."
"Come in," said Bunny.
"Tell us about it."

20

She grabbed her notepad.
"Which balloons? Where?"
asked Jack.
"The ones I tie
to the front of the store,"
said Mr. Paris,
sitting down.

"I always tie four balloons outside
in the morning.
And somebody keeps taking them."
"Hmmm," said Bunny.
She wrote down:

4 balloons outside

"What do the balloons look like?"
Bunny asked.

"They're green and yellow,"
said Mr. Paris,
"to match my delivery truck.
And they're tied with blue ribbon."
Bunny wrote down:

green and yellow
blue ribbon

"And do they disappear every day?"
she asked.
"No—only on Fridays,"
said Mr. Paris.
"Hmmm," said Bunny.
She wrote down:

disappear on Fridays

Mr. Paris's Toy Store
4 balloons outside
green and yellow
blue ribbon
disappear on
Fridays

"And when did this start happening?"
Bunny asked.

"This fall," said Mr. Paris.

"No one ever bothered them
in the summer."

"Hmmm," said Bunny again.

She wrote down:

fall, not summer

"And do you have any
Android Attack action figures?"
asked Jack.
"What's that got to do
with anything?" asked Bunny.
"Nothing," said Jack.
"I just like them."

"Concentrate on the case, Jack,"
said Bunny.

"Right," said Jack. "Mr. Paris,
on your way through the store
to tie up the balloons,
which are now missing,
did you ever pass any
Android Attack action figures?"

"Jack!" said Bunny.

"What?" asked Jack.

"Mr. Paris," said Bunny, "don't worry.

We'll solve this case.

You can count on us."

She gave Jack a look.

"Well, one of us will, anyway," she said.

"Hey," said Jack.

"Thank you, Bunny. Thank you, Jack,"

said Mr. Paris.

"I knew I could depend on you."

Mr. Paris walked to the door.

"By the way, Jack," he said,

"I have seven

Android Attack action figures.

And they come with accessories."

"COOL!" said Jack.

Bunny just sighed.

Chapter 3
The Turtles

"Okay," said Bunny

after Mr. Paris left.

"Let's look at our clues."

"Okay," said Jack.

They read the clues.

"Green and yellow.

Blue ribbon.

Fridays in the fall," said Bunny.

"TGIF," said Jack.

"What?" asked Bunny.

" 'Thank goodness it's Friday,' "
said Jack. "TGIF.
Didn't you say that
when you were in school?"
"No," said Bunny. "I said,
'Gee, I have a ton of homework.' "

"Oh," said Jack. "Too bad.

I said it.

Because Fridays meant fun.

Movies, cookouts, ball games,

swim—"

"WAIT!" said Bunny. "THAT'S IT!"

"What's it?" asked Jack.

"Ball games," said Bunny.

"In the fall. On Fridays."

Jack thought a minute.

"Right!" he said. "And just as
Mr. Paris wants colors
that match his truck, . . ."
"School kids want colors
that match their team," said Bunny.
"I'll bet somebody
is taking those balloons
to Friday night football games."
"Right," said Jack.
"Let's think about school colors,"
said Bunny.

"There's the Westover Weasels."

"Red and gray," said Jack.

"The Southside Seagulls."

"Blue and white," said Jack.

"And the Tarrytown Turtles."

"GREEN AND YELLOW!"

said Jack.

"Bingo," said Bunny.

"We're going to a game."

"Yay, team!" said Jack.

Chapter 4
Solved

Jack picked up Bunny
on Friday night.
He was wearing a turtle shirt,
a turtle hat,
and a turtle scarf.
He also had a pom-pom.
"We have to fit in,"
said Jack.
"Right," said Bunny.

"Do you want the hat?" asked Jack.

"No," said Bunny.

"The scarf?"

"No," said Bunny.

"Well, you can't have the shirt,"
said Jack. "I'll catch cold."

"I want the pom-pom," said Bunny.

"But the pom-pom's the most fun,"
said Jack. "I thought
you'd want the hat."
"Let's share the pom-pom,"
said Bunny.
"Okay," said Jack.
"I get it first."

Football
Field

"No, me," said Bunny.

"Me," said Jack.

"Jack, you said you'd share,"
said Bunny.

"I have trouble
sharing pom-poms," said Jack.

"Oh, all right," said Bunny.

"I'll wear the hat."

She put it on.

"Bunny, you look MARVELOUS!"
said Jack.

"Ha," said Bunny.

Jack and Bunny went to see
the Tarrytown Turtles play
the Southside Seagulls.
They sat on the Turtles' side.
Everything was green and yellow,
including four balloons.

"Look!" said Jack.

A young turtle was holding

the balloons and cheering.

"How do we know they belong

to Mr. Paris?" asked Jack.

"Mr. Paris said he tied them together

with blue ribbon,"

said Bunny.

"Let's go see," said Jack.

They stood behind the turtle.

"Bingo," said Bunny.

"Now what?" asked Jack.

"Well," said Bunny.

"He's just a kid.

We don't want to scare him

or make him cry."

"Right," said Jack. "Wow,

do you smell that popcorn?"

"That's *it*!" said Bunny.

"Oh, good, I'm starving," said Jack.

"No, I mean we'll use *popcorn*.

We'll write a note and stick it

in a popcorn cup," said Bunny.

"Great," said Jack. "You write the note

while I get the popcorn. It's my *JOB*!"

"Ha," said Bunny.

While Jack got three cups of popcorn,

Bunny wrote a little note. It said:

*Please don't take balloons
from the toy store,
or you know what.*
Santa Claus

Jack and Bunny gave the young turtle

their extra cup of popcorn.

Then they left.

"What did the note say?"

asked Jack.

"It said, 'This raccoon eats too much,'"

said Bunny.

"Very funny," said Jack.

"By the way, are you hungry?

Want to get another snack?"

"Well, I have some apples at home,"

said Bunny.

"You mean the kind that don't itch?"

asked Jack.

"Yes," said Bunny.

"Cool," said Jack.

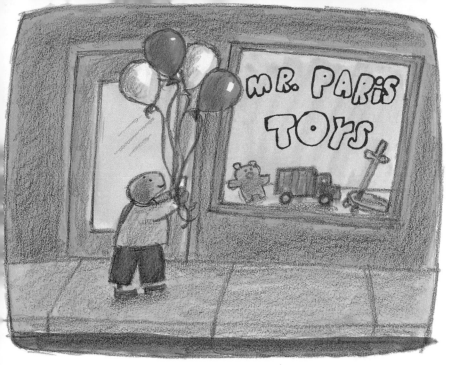

On the way home
Bunny and Jack rode past
Mr. Paris's store.
A nice young turtle
was tying some balloons
to the door.
"Case closed," said Bunny.
"TGIF," said Jack.
"What?" asked Bunny.

47

"Thank goodness I'm fantastic,"
said Jack.

"Silly," said Bunny.

"You bet!" said Jack.